You're a CrocaGator!

by Kenny Rager

Illustrated by
Patti Brassard Jefferson

Halo
Publishing International

TO LALCHAN

Kenny Rager

ISBN: 978-1-61244-279-2
Library of Congress Control Number: 2014914421

Printed in the United States of America

Publishing International
www.halopublishing.com

Published by Halo Publishing International
1100 NW Loop 410
Suite 700 - 176
San Antonio, Texas 78213
Toll Free 1-877-705-9647
www.halopublishing.com
www.holapublishing.com
e-mail: contact@halopublishing.com

Introduction

You're a CrocaGator was inspired by a comment made by my illustrator, Patti Brassard Jefferson, while discussing the illustrations for a new book of mine. I told her I had decided to use alligators, not crocodiles, as the characters in the book. She replied that she would need to study the differences before doing the artwork because she could not tell an alligator from a crocodile and referred to them both as "CrocaGators."

I told her I loved the term and I wanted to use it somehow in one of my poems. That night I found the inspiration to write a poem about a crocodile named CrocaSonny, who falls in love with GatorSissy, a beautiful alligator he spots across the creek.

CrocaSonny and GatorSissy represent a mixed family like many others throughout the world. This is especially true in America, where due to the immigration of peoples from other countries, we come from a wide variety and blend of cultures and ethnic backgrounds. In a way, we are all "CrocaGators."

Our own diversity creates social and family issues for both children and adults. My hope is that parents will share this children's book with their families to promote awareness and discussion of issues our mixed society faces today. I hope it helps children realize that, although we are all different and unique, we are also very similar with a great deal in common. We can celebrate our individuality and still live together in harmony with God.

I intend to use the "CrocaGator" in a series of books to address childhood and family issues. In the near future be on the look out for books about: a step CrocaGator, a baby CrocaGator, a handicapped CrocaGator and a bullied CrocaGator, to name a few.

Let me know what issues the CrocaGator can explore for you at my website www.kennyspoems.com. While you are there, you can also buy more CrocaGator stuffed animals, t-shirts, books and other poems.

Note: In reality crocodiles and alligators cannot mate as they are not from the same species; they are as different as a lion and an elephant. They have not had a common ancestor for 65 million years so you won't be seeing any CrocaGators outside of this book.

4

Once upon a swampy river lived a crocodile family of three.
There was Crocamommy, Crocadaddy and little Crocasonny.

The three of them swam the river and hunted for food to eat.
They relaxed in the shade along the banks to avoid the heat.

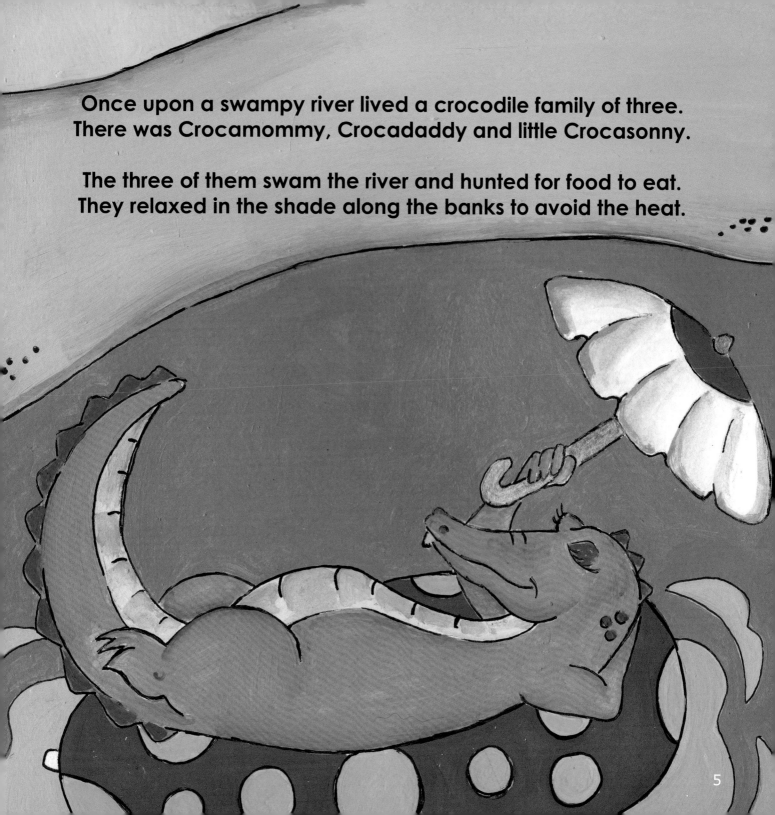

Crocasonny learned to hunt and was fast on all four feet.
He could smell a meal a mile away and was very discreet.

His mom and dad were proud of his growth into a fine big croc.
They knew the day was near, when he would have to leave
their block.

One warm evening Crocasonny
went fishing for a treat to eat.
He explored far down the river,
way past his ordinary beat.

8

He noticed another croc moving on the other side of a creek.
Curious to make a friend, he swam across for a closer peek.

9

When he got there he was surprised to find a croc like no other.
As he approached he could tell she was a girl like his mother.

Her skin was a pretty color and she had the cutest short nose.
Crocasonny thought she was so beautiful, he almost froze.

She liked his narrow nose
and found him handsome and strong.

They took off for a swim and discovered they really got along.

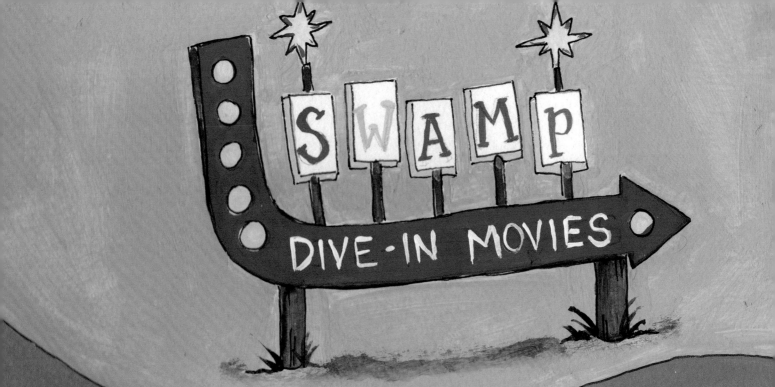

As they got to know each other, she explained she was a gator.
He admitted his mom and dad were crocs a few moments later.

They did not look the same, but they fell in love with each other.
It mattered not to them, until the day he met her father.

Gatordaddy said
"This guy is a croc, and I forbid you to see him."

16

That's when Gatormommy stepped
in and said, "Let's all go for a swim."

Dad settled down when he saw Crocasonny made Gatorsissy happy.
The next day they swam the river to meet Croc's mom and pappy.

They were different, but nice and they all swam the same river.
They ate alike and were all hunted by the same tribe upriver.

SWAMP MEAT

GATOR TATER SALAD

19

As Gatorsissy and Crocasonny
talked it over a question arose.
What if we have kids some day,
will they have a funny nose?

20

They agreed to proudly say,
"You were blessed by the Creator.
You got the very best of both of us. So

You're a CrocaGator."

Dedicated to Lyndsey House

Proceeds from the sale of every book go to support the soon-to-open "Lyndsey House" in Fort Myers, Florida. Lyndsey House is a shelter for women and women with children operated by the Fort Myers Rescue Mission.

The Fort Myers Rescue Mission was founded in 1973 and operates a men's homeless shelter at 6900 Mission Lane, Fort Myers, Florida. They are funded entirely by private donations and churches in the community and accept no financial aid from the government. They clothe, shelter, feed, help, minister and counsel thousands of homeless and needy people annually. For more information, see fortmyersrescuemission.org.

In 2013, the Mission approached me about donating the use of a 20 room house that we own for use as their women's shelter. We gladly granted their request and they agreed to name it in honor of my daughter, Lyndsey Grace, who died in 2011 at the age of 22 from diabetes complications. Lyndsey loved to help people in need. It would have been her fondest desire to see our community have a Lyndsey House.